HOW TO LOSE A HIPPOPATAMUS

Tippy

To order additional copies of this book, contact:
Xlibris
844-714-8691
www.Xlibris.com
Orders@Xlibris.com

ISBN: Softcover   978-1-6698-7132-3
            Hardcover   978-1-6698-7130-9
            EBook   978-1-6698-7131-6

Print information available on the last page

Rev. date: 03/21/2023

Dedication

I WOULD LIKE TO DEDICATE THIS
BOOK TO MY GRANDCHILDREN; RYAN,
CRYSTAL, JACOB, HEIDI AND BELLA

One day, Tippy the clown joined the circus. Tippy always wanted to be in the circus. He liked to juggle, do tricks, and make children laugh.

In the circus there were many talented families
from all over the world, including many animals;
elephants, lions, tigers, horses, monkeys,
dogs, and many more.

One of the animals in the circus was a Hippo named Elmo.

One day when it was time to move the circus, Dino, the driver of the truck, asked Tippy if he would be his shotgun, a term used in the circus to help guide the driver to the next town.

Tippy agreed and off they went to the next town.

Bright red arrows are posted along the road to show the way to the next town for another performance by the circus.

Along the way Tippy asked Dino if they could stop by a friend's house to visit. Dino said he is not supposed to go off the route with the arrows. Tippy said it wasn't that far off, so they went.

When they arrived at Tippy's friend's house, Tippy asked Dino to wait in the truck, and said the visit wouldn't be long.

There was no place to park but the street, so Dino and Elmo waited for Tippy with a Concerned look.

While Tippy was visiting his friend, a police car pulled up and noticed a big red circus truck parked in the middle of the street.

The look on the policeman's face when he realized there was a live hippo in the truck.

"You can't park a hippo in the city!' yelled the policeman to Dino. So Dino had to move the truck.

Tippy finally stepped out of the house to his surprise, Elmo and his truck were gone!

Tippy's heart began to beat very fast! After some pondering, Tippy realized he had to get back to the circus, so he began his long journey back.

After several rides and long walks, Tippy arrived back to the circus early the following morning.

Upon returning, the circus manager spotted Tippy and yelled out to him; "Tippy! Where is the hippo truck?" Not knowing what to say, Tippy exclaimed, "I don't know!"

Tippy had lost a hippopotamus!

Later that morning

Everyone saw a tow truck pulling Elmo and the hippo truck onto the lot. The truck had broken down!

Tippy went to see Elmo; Elmo was doing well and was safe now. It wasn't funny then, but, looking back, after all those years, Tippy would try to tell someone he lost a hippo once; they either laughed or didn't believe him. Tippy promised the manager he would never go off the route again. Tippy and Elmo lived happily ever after.

Tippy The Clown Gallery

44

45

Printed in the United States
by Baker & Taylor Publisher Services